Joseph Matthias Jones

Dream-Visions of Christmastide

Joseph Matthias Jones

Dream-Visions of Christmastide

ISBN/EAN: 9783337380823

Printed in Europe, USA, Canada, Australia, Japan

Cover: Foto ©Andreas Hilbeck / pixelio.de

More available books at **www.hansebooks.com**

DREAM-VISIONS

OF

CHRISTMASTIDE

BY

JOSEPH MATTHIAS JONES

" MEMORY OF THE FAR-GONE YEARS HATH BLOWN
UPON ME LIKE THE BREATH OF PASSION, AND SAILED
ME INTO A SEA OF VAST DREAMS, WHEREBY EACH
WAVE IS AT ONCE A VISION AND A MELODY."

" The moss-stained marble rests
O'er the lips my lips pressed
In their bloom ;
And the names I loved to hear
Have been carved for many a year
On the tomb."

Consecration

GRATEFUL FOR ALL THY TENDER
MINISTRY TO ME, IN SHADE AND SHINE,
IN GRIEF AND GLADNESS, I CONSE-
CRATE THESE LEAVES WITH TEARS;
ENTWINE THEM WITH LILIES FROM
THE GARDEN OF MY GRATITUDE, AND
LOVINGLY SING TO THEE, SWEET
PRINCE OF PEACE.

Christmastide.

Dreaming, we float on Memory's wings to realms of far-gone years.

Voice after voice; vision after vision pass before us. Softly the dusk falls; night crowds on us; the fire-glow fades to dull, gray ashes: curtains are drawn; the bed invites: sleep gently tips eyelids and wooes to rest—and to dreams.

Between the eveningtide and the morningtide one traveler has invaded the homes of Christendom. Ah, Santa, thou art a generous Prince, for thy trade is to give and make happy. May thy smiling face never grow older; thy snowy beard less glossy; thy fat hands less cunning;

thy storehouse less full. May thy whip have a golden stock and a silken lash to speed thy gallant reindeer to expectant hearts. We see thy form and face only through the dream shadows, but we hear the echoes of thy sleigh and the merry song of thy bells, and the old feel young again, the strong stronger still, and childhood leaps for joy.

Thy coming makes this the day of days for the young ; the time when they taste the sweetest sweets of all the year.

A Dream Vision rises, and we are borne back through the dead centuries. A star has risen and its wondrous light floods the land. The wise men catch its beams and quickly mount and speed over the

Syrian plain. Awe-struck and silent they journey through the still hours of the night, with eyes fixed on the star whose light paints in colors of ravishing beauty the fair face of the gentle Virgin-Mother, on whose blue veined, lily-white bosom nestles The Babe.

Another Dream-Vision bears us to the Christmastides of the long-ago,

ere youth had closed his golden door
—the time when " we waded knee-
deep in the stream of Memory that
flowed from the land of youth—
when the prophet-dreams of youth
sang only of joy and victory." The
firelight flings quivering warmth
about our chamber, and in pensive,
saddened mood we recall the vanished past. We enter the old home

—now, alas! crumbling to decay and the home of strangers—where we companied with adored ones whose voices have long been hushed in dreamless sleep. O! the charms of that home, and the tenderness of affection that were ours in "the days that are no more." Again we sip sweets from lips and feel the warm embrace of those who were the idols of our hearts. We stand once more in the hallowed shrine—the mother's room—and suspended from the mantelpiece over the dear old fireplace—the bright wood fire gave out its soft glow and comfort in those faraway sweet, sweet days—we see the row of stockings, and then we catch the echoes of shout and laugh of little brothers and sisters as they tumble rosy and happy

out of bed ; and then a mist gathers

upon our eyes to blur the vision as

we remember that some of those

precious little ones were taken from

our home, and our broken hearts by

the call of the Christmas-Born, and

are sleeping yonder in the Voiceless

City. If, then, our hearts be sad-

dened by the remembrance of the

vanished days that were fraught with melancholy partings, they are also softened and purified, and all coldness and selfishness are banished from our thoughts on this holy Christmas day. Pity and compassion—sweet and gentle graces—reign supreme, while Charity stands erect in peerless beauty, with no stain upon her spotless robes, and we bend

to her beneficent commands ; queen
of graces, linking the heart of Him
the Good to the heart of Man the
Generous. To-day we are lost to
self, and forget our own deep griefs
and find our chiefest happiness in
ministering to those more wretched
than ourselves. "We feel the sense
of obligation and of wrong—pity
for those who toil and weep—tears

for the imprisoned and despised—
love for the noble living--reverence
for the generous dead—and in heart
the rapture of a high resolve."

The Voice again sings to the heart
bidding a remembrance that the
year now nearing its close has been
rough to many ; the sky of hope
obscured : the soul's light clouded
by bitter griefs. Then we catch the

.

soft notes of His voice—"Be merciful," and we turn with succoring hand, and cheery voice, and sunny smile to His desolate ones; to the widow in her abode of poverty, with the shadow of despair her constant companion; to the man once vigorous, now wasting under fatal malady, with no ray of hope to cheer his path to the tomb; to the crippled child—ah this is the sad picture—lying in orphan ward of hospital, about whose pale, sweet face few smiles have played, yet beautiful withal, the Great Artist having tinted that face with the supreme touch that melts and wins the beholder's heart—Innocence. We look through tears upon the little sufferer—august in her purity and

helplessness—with tenderest compassion. "What hand but would
a loving garland cull for one so
frail and beautiful."

On this holy day the Voice bids
us comfort and cheer those bending
under the stroke of some great
agony. "While we may not drown
grief in oblivion, we can dignify it
by hope; while we may not calm

the despairing soul by pointing it down to the grave of resignation, we can turn it from the darkness of the tomb to the brightness of the stars."

"He who has not felt in his soul the strong throbs of Love and Grief, and has not seen the things of this life, and read the hearts of men and women by this double light, has seen but little, and knows but little of the human heart."

To-day we recall those in homes where sunbeams enter not; a noble father agonizes over his wayward, wandering son; a sweet and loving mother mourns a once pure and affectionate daughter—now lost in the city's dens of shame. Their wretchedness being all the more intensified as they see smiles and happiness in other homes; and as these broken-hearted ones move in loneliness of soul, Compassion turns us to weep with them—what more can we do?

" Touched by Compassion's hand, the wayside weed
 Becomes a fragrant flower! the lowliest reed
  Beside the stream is clothed with beauty.
 It sings of love, its flame illumes
 The darkest of lone cottage rooms."

And thus the Dream-Visions and

Dream-Voices come to us, on the day fraught with so much mingled joy and sorrow, sunshine and shadow ; we bow in mournful revery—for our thoughts are of our scattered living and our gathered dead—and then a stir in the graveyard of Memory, the slumbering thoughts rise again, and the full omnipotence of affection returns to the heart and streams out from the beautiful faces of those we loved—and have lost awhile. The one supreme and beauteous face that rises out of the crystal depths of Memory, before which we linger with rapturous joy and sadness, the face of the one of all the world the sweetest and best beloved, is that of the patient and gentle mother, who watched our babyhood and childhood and youth with angelic tenderness, and from the far-away Valley of Bliss float to us the echoes of her voice, in melody sweeter than the sweetest carol of bird, and as we look up toward the Celestial Country, her bright home, and ours to be, we recall her radiant presence as she moved among us, and wonder how it was

possible for us to have survived our
grief when she said her last farewell
and took her flight; and then
" through the hallowed glory of the
past more precious seems that face,
more beautiful, more divinely fair,
as we decay, as we grow old, more
dearly loved for the tender memories
it brings." Once more we see the
form and face of the venerable

father who wrought for us in his days of manly vigor; and now there troop before us a cluster of darling little ones, brothers and sisters, with whom we walked in the cool of the evening of life's early dawn. Another picture of noble beauty and dignity rises in view—the sweet faced beloved old grandmother, sitting in the corner of the old family room.

O! the voices crowd upon us, some echoing happy marriage bells, others the mournful funeral dirge. Only at Christmastide do we hold the talisman which brings the perished years back to us; then it is we remember the sweets and blessings of life, and we strive to banish sad thoughts as our lips move in prayer—we pour out our gratitude to the Great Giver for the gift of Christian parents, a Christian home, and many Christian friends; nor do we forget to fervently plead for all mankind—that He will send the Christian teacher to the whole human race to tell of the gentle Nazarene.

In the town, as in the country, this holy day flings beams of gladness.

The first snowflake falls, then others, and soon the earth turns white. The jingle of sleigh bells cuts through the frosty air; merry notes ring out from pedestrians hurrying along the streets, bearing beautiful things for loved ones at home. The bright green Christmas tree is planted in the biggest room, and it yields a wonderful harvest for the little folk

in a single night.   In the country
home are gathered the kin of gener-
ations—ah, what picture so lovely as
that of the Christmas reunion in the
old country home !   The big wood
fire burns with a proud and con-
scious glow, as it flings a light soft
as a dream of peace about the forms
and faces gathered there.   The rooms
and halls are gracefully festooned

with masses of evergreen and holly

bright with berries ; white roses and

violets fill the air with grateful odors;

then come apples and nuts and

sparkling cider—brewed from blush-

ing and golden fruit from the old

orchard ; faces glow ; hearts are

happy ; the wild racket of the little

ones makes the walls ring again ;

story-telling follows, and from the

lips of the patriarch of this happy circle comes a story whose sweet lesson touches every heart :

The Beautiful Hand.

There was a dispute among three ladies as to which had the most beautiful hand. One sat by a stream and dipped her hand into the water and held it up; another plucked strawberries until the ends of her fingers were pink; and another gathered violets

until her hands were fragrant. An old
and haggard woman passing by, asked :

"Who will give me a gift, for I am
poor?"

All three denied her; but another
who sat near, unwashed in the stream,
unstained with fruit, unadorned with
flowers, gave her a little gift, and satis-
fied the poor woman. And then she
asked them what was the dispute. They
told her, and lifted up before her
their beautiful hands.

"Beautiful, indeed," said she when she saw them. But when they asked her which was the most beautiful, she said :

" It is not the hand that is washed in the brook ; it is not the hand that is tipped with red ; it is not the hand that is garlanded with fragrant flowers —but the hand that gives to the poor is the most beautiful ! "

As she said these words her wrinkles fled, her staff was thrown away, and

she stood before them an angel from
heaven, with authority to decide the
question in dispute. And that decis-
ion has stood the test of all time.

Outside the wind howls and sends
the snow in drifts against the window panes ; the cattle are snugly
housed ; the rabbits are warm under
the bushes ; the birds are sheltered
under the eaves of the barn ; and

so, without and within the old country home all is joy and peace and comfort.

Once more the echoes of Christmastide come to us from a city vision, and His sweet and pleading voice is heard:

" There is a doorway in a narrow street,
    And close beside that door a broken stair,
        And then a low, dark room;
        The room is bare.
        But in a corner lies

A worn-out form upon a hard straw bed—

No pillow underneath the aching head—

A face grown wan with suffering, and a hand

Scarce strong enough to reach the small dry crust

    That lies upon the chair.

    Go in, for I am there;

I have been waiting wearily in that cold room—

    Waiting long, lonely hours—

    Waiting for thee to come

And minister to my suffering one."

And now we catch another Dream

Voice which whispers of our failures

and our triumphs in life ; of words

and acts of ours that gave pain to

others, and we beg our Father to
pardon us and to heal the wounds
we made ; we recall words and acts
of others that put sorrow in our
heart, and we invoke a Father's
blessing upon them, and beg Him to
forgive them and give us back their
friendship and their love. We remember—remember but to bless—
those who came to us with loving

succor when pain and grief swept
their billows over us. We also see
rising before us the sad eyes, patient
faces, wasting forms, of those to
whom we gave the soft word, the
tender touch, the sunny smile, the
cup of strength, when their griefs
bore heaviest ; and then we resolve
to succor and cheer other suffering,
burdened souls—"not to keep the

alabaster box of love and tenderness sealed up until our friends are
dead, but to put some sweetness in
their lives; to speak the cheering
words while their ears can hear
them, that their hearts can be
thrilled and made happy by them;
the kind things we are wont to say
when they are dead and gone we
we will say now, before they go; the

flowers we mean to send to their coffins we will send now, to brighten and scenten their homes before they leave them—that they may behold their beauty and inhale their fragrance, remembering that flowers on the coffin are but seen by the living, their perfume only grateful to the living, that they put no sweetness in the nostrils of the dead."

" We wound the living heart, yet clip the briers

From roses that we lay in pulseless hands;

We build for frozen hearts our tardy fires,

And pour love's chalice upon graveyard sands."

Still dreaming, I was borne to a palatial home. It was the sweet spring-time, and without nature spread her beauties and her glories. Tender, plaintive notes of forest warblers quivered on the golden air. Within, wealth and culture graced with art's choicest treasures; through

stained windows streamed a mellow

light, while sweetest and fairest

flowers lent wondrous beauty and

fragrance to the scene. In a costly

casket, embellished with solid silver

trappings, lay one that had just

reached manhood's proudest stage :

who had quaffed deeply at the

world's fountain of pleasures and

defilements: reared in a home of luxury by those who valued the glittering things of time above the fadeless things of eternity. As I looked upon the frozen face, classic in its manly beauty, I heard a cry that chilled my blood, such a cry as can come alone from a heart tortured by remorse and bereft of hope, and then turned and met the glare of a

woman's eye—the proud and worldly
mother of the dead—and as I stood
under the shadow of the saddened
scene, in the presence of the mated
mysteries, Life and Death, there
swept athwart the chamber in letters
black as the raven's wing the appall-
ing sentence—

DIED WITHOUT HOPE—LOST!
—and as these words vanished from

my view, there smote upon my ear

the mournful toll of distant bell, and

then a darkness, dense and awful,

drowned my vision and my dream.

Again I dreamed and was borne to

a modest cottage home, whose hum-

ble dwellers had often felt the pinch

of poverty.   Without, the air was

laden with fragrance of simple

flowers, and doors and windows

wreathed with trailing vines. With-

in, all was plain, but clean and sweet.

Death had entered here, and in a

wooden coffin lay a manly youth, the

seal of peaceful repose stamped upon

his marble face. As I stood in the

shaded light of this hushed and sol-

emn scene, my ear caught a woman's

soft, low cry—the cry of the gentle

Christian mother of the dead—and

as I met her gaze I read in eye and
on face that sorrow's wound had
been touched with healing by the
Master's hand; and then, in letters
of radiant light, there moved across
the room the words of comfort—

DIED IN THE FAITH—SAVED!
—and from the old church over the
way there came strains of triumph-
ant song, and there above the dark-

ness of the dead shone Hope's bright star, and then I awoke to find my chamber suffused with soft beams of the morning sun.

Back of the hand that writes these lines lies a heart that throbs in tender, loyal love for childhood and youth. As I stand in the mellow autumn of my life, at that hour " When night is not yet, and day is no more," and look back over the traveled way,

recounting the history of one sad

and suffering heart, and there come

in review before tear-blurred eyes

the multiform scenes in the pilgrim-

age of one wan and weary life; scenes

at once the saddest and sweetest; the

most joyous and the most mournful;

and remember what childhood and

youth must encounter as the years

crowd on toward manhood—much,
oh, so much, that will wring tears
from the eye, and pierce the soul
with agony—the warmest compassion of my heart sweeps to you in
flood-tide fullness, oh, innocent and
adorable childhood. Would that I
could compass you as with a shield,
and hedge you from the dangers and
impurities that will woo you from

duty's path. Would that I might impress you with the truth—The cleaner the living the braver the heart, the braver the heart the nobler the life, the nobler the life the whiter the soul, the whiter the soul the more peaceful the end when the curtain rolls down for the last time on earth.

Another Vision rises, and we are carried back through the ages to a scene of barbarous cruelty and Christian martyrdom. Imperial Rome has turned her populace to the Colosseum, which stands in its pristine splendor. Pillars and arches of the mighty structure are adorned with rich colors of the Orient; the cope of the balustrade mounted with parian and bronze statues of rulers, philosophers, warriors, poets, orators and masters of art. Richly embroidered awnings protect the royal quarters from the mid-day heat; burnished shields and spears of warrior legions reflect back the brilliant light, and golden eagles, kissed by the soft Italian sun, are borne aloft like glories in the air. A Christian convert, a Greek maiden, torn from her home by Rome's mail-clad hand, enters the arena. Against her pearl-white brow tenderly beats the breath of the Eternal Morning. Her clear eye of faith penetrates the veil and catches a glimpse of the green pastures and still waters in the land of Jerusalem the Golden.

Modest, yet courageous, supported by a strength born of saintly devotion, she presents a picture of classic and pathetic beauty, ready to yield her sweet young life, that she may proclaim her love for Him who lay in Bethlehem's Manger. Bolts are thrown back, a trumpet signals, and with hungry growl the wild beasts spring in; flesh is mangled, blood flows, bones are crushed, and a pure soul is white-winged for flight to Paradise.

We marvel—and pity as we mar-vel—that any can refuse belief in Him for whom the gentle maiden died. We wonder how any human heart can fix its faith and affection solely on finite things in a world that contains no satisfying portion for the soul: where the blighting forces of sin touch but to consume. The Voice whispers that when the body and soul come to part company at the portal of the tomb, happy only will be he who has anchored his hope on the Great Martyr; whose riches await him in the Celestial Beyond. Only such a one will find cheer in the hour when he draws nearer and nearer to the calm Sea of Eternity. The Voice sings of a purer, gladder stream than any that flows from the

fountain source of wealth and honors
and the fading things of earth—a
stream that rises in the soul of Faith
and glides gently on to Heaven's
Crystal Waters.

And now, as we sit alone in our
silent chamber, the fire glow grows
paler and paler and then fades away;
the faithful old clock ticks measure-
ment to the fast dying hours of

the blessed Christmastide; Memory weaves the tangled threads of the past into dream-pictures; the perished years float back to us, freighted with the dark and the bright, the visions and voices grow sadder and sweeter, and more ineffably tender and radiant and holy; before our sweeping and earnest gaze lies spread out the wide domain of all our wanderings, from

the warm white dawn of the morningtide—the sun kissing the silken
curls of childhood, to the gray dusk
of eventide—the shadows of night
falling over the silver locks of age.

With loving gratitude we remember the countless blessings which
have come to us from the Father's
hand; First and before all and above
all, the holy, gentle child of His heart;

He whose coming made human life and liberty securer; the home-life dearer and sweeter; the hearts of men and women purer, truer, braver; the star of hope shine brighter.

The wonderful depths of motherly love; the marvelous sweetness of wifely devotion; the fragrant kiss of the little child and the little child's happy prattle; the entrancing beauties of nature—her peaceful valleys, quiet woodlands, lofty mountains, crystal waters, the fresh green of spring, the rich glories of summer, the mellow splendors of autumn, the joys of winter's Christmas cheer: the journeys made amid scenes of exceeding beauty by day and under glories of bending skies by night; the enchantments of literature, and

music, and art; the thrill of ecstasy
born of the friendship of the good
and true, the brave and noble among
men and women: If these be links
in the chain that binds us to this life,
making it sweet betimes, how often
have the links been torn asunder
and the chain lain broken at our feet!

Mournfully we recall the rugged
steps and thorny paths; the weary

marches through stress and storm, sacrifice and pain; ceaseless toil palsying and numbing the hand's cunning, and grief's tears burning and dimming the eye's vision; the hurtling thrusts of the blade of adversity; the combats with manifold temptations; the cruel frown of the friend who counted our thoughtless error of the head as an intentional

wrong of the heart; the temples of sadness entered through portals draped
with mourning; the fountain of tears
in which we bathed; the frosts that
fell about our home, chilling the
tender bud and withering the lovely
flower—sealing the lips of the child
and closing the eyes of the mother,
leaving us alone in the dark chamber
with silence and with death, and our

desolate soul to wander ever after through rayless night.

With the shadows growing more ominous as the years crowd on, the lonely soul crying out "Why linger amid the glooms here, when splendid lights invite you yonder?" the eye looks through the window of its Faith, toward the home where

the dew of youth ever lingers
on the cheek; the radiance of
immortality lights the brow; where
tears are unknown; where no blur
falls on the rose, no blight on
the lily, no chill deadens the vio-
let's perfume; where strife and
wrath, pain nor sickness ever
come; where no hurtful thing
ever enters; where voices are for-

ever sweet and faces forever fair; where the touch of imperishable loveliness rests upon all.

Being hard pressed in the battle, wan and weary, tired of feet and wounded in heart, storm-tossed and far from home, with earth's stains upon our garments and its sorrows surging to our soul, we yearn for the White Land of Peace, where we may look into those tender eyes that closed on the cross; lay our tired hand in the dear hand that was pierced for us; listen to the melody of that voice that echoed charity, compassion, healing and peace through the valleys, across the plains, over the hills and across the waters of Palestine; and there join the loved of our heart, and hand in hand with them, wander along the quiet waters, and through the perfumed pastures as long as eternity, resting, betimes, beneath the soft shade of the Tree of Life, and find that tranquil repose for the soul we here have sought for, striven for, yearned for in vain ; and as the Dream takes wing and bears us toward white hands that are seen beckoning us home, our listening ears catch words, in accents of melting tenderness,

"SAD AND WEARY OF EARTH COME TO ME AND REST."

As the echos of these restful, comforting words die softly away, my dream is broken, and I awake to meet a flood of golden light that flashes across the snow-drifts,

through my window, into my

chamber, and behold it is

CHRISTMAS MORNING.

TO THEE,
O SWEET READER.
I REVEAL THE SECRETS OF
MY HEART—
ITS SADNESS, ITS LONGINGS AND ITS FAITH.
I AM THY FRIEND!
ART THOU MY FRIEND?
IF THOU ART
GENTLY I LAY MY HAND IN THY HAND,
POUR THE LOVE OF MY HEART
INTO THY HEART,
AND TENDERLY BID THEE
FAREWELL.